ART in Different Places

Robin Johnson

Crabtree Publishing Company
www.crabtreebooks.com

Learning About Our GLOBAL COMMUNITY

Author: Robin Johnson

Publishing plan research and development: Reagan Miller

Substantive editor: Reagan Miller

Editor: Janine Deschenes

Notes to educators: Janine Deschenes

Proofreader: Ellen Rodger

Design: Samara Parent

Photo research: Robin Johnson & Samara Parent

Production coordinator and prepress technician: Samara Parent

Print coordinator: Margaret Amy Salter

Photographs:
Alamy: ©Tuul and Bruno Morandi: contents (bottom); ©Sherab: p6; ©David R. Frazier Photolibrary, Inc.: p11 (bottom); ©Tibor Bognar: p13 (top); ©Paul Kingsley: p13 (bottom); ©Irene Abdou: p16 (bottom); ©Jake Lyell: p18 (bottom); ©Judy Bellah: p21 (top); ©UpperCut Images: p21 (bottom)
Getty: ©TORU YAMANAKA: p12 (bottom); ©Soltan Frédéric: p20
Shutterstock: ©Authentic Creations: title page; ©Michal Knitl: p7 (top) ; ©Ilia Torlin: p7 (bottom); ©Popova Valeriya: p8; ©Sophie McAulay: p9 (top); ©Vladimir Melnik: p10 (top); ©Artur Bogacki: p10 (bottom); ©Sergey Uryadnikov: p15 (top); ©kvika: p17 (top); ©Dmitry Chulov: p19 (bottom)
Superstock: ©Toby Adamson / Axiom Photographic/Design Pics: cover
All other images by Shutterstock

Front cover: A woman holds an African woven basket.

Title page: An ice sculpture of a giant hand on display at a festival in Poland.

Contents page: Pottery from Morocco (top left); girls with henna designs on their hands (bottom left)

Library and Archives Canada Cataloguing in Publication

Johnson, Robin (Robin R.), author
Art in different places / Robin Johnson.

(Learning about our global community)
Includes index.
Issued in print and electronic formats.
ISBN 978-0-7787-3654-7 (hardcover).--ISBN 978-0-7787-3663-9 (softcover).--ISBN 978-1-4271-1965-0 (HTML)

1. Art--Juvenile literature. 2. Art appreciation--Juvenile literature. I. Title.

N7440.J64 2017 j700 C2017-905144-X
C2017-905145-8

Library of Congress Cataloging-in-Publication Data

Names: Johnson, Robin (Robin R.), author.
Title: Art in different places / Robin Johnson.
Description: New York : Crabtree Publishing Company, 2017. | Series: Learning about our global community | Includes index. |
Identifiers: LCCN 2017042525 (print) | LCCN 2017042724 (ebook) | ISBN 9781427119650 (Electronic HTML) | ISBN 9780778736547 (reinforced library binding : alk. paper) | ISBN 9780778736639 (pbk. : alk. paper)
Subjects: LCSH: Art and society--Juvenile literature.
Classification: LCC N72.S6 (ebook) | LCC N72.S6 J59 2017 (print) | DDC 701/.03--dc23
LC record available at https://lccn.loc.gov/2017042525

Crabtree Publishing Company

Printed in the USA/102017/CG20170907

www.crabtreebooks.com 1-800-387-7650

Published in Canada
Crabtree Publishing
616 Welland Ave.
St. Catharines, Ontario
L2M 5V6

Published in the United States
Crabtree Publishing
PMB 59051
350 Fifth Avenue, 59th Floor
New York, New York 10118

Published in the United Kingdom
Crabtree Publishing
Maritime House
Basin Road North, Hove
BN41 1WR

Published in Australia
Crabtree Publishing
3 Charles Street
Coburg North
VIC 3058

Contents

Our Global Community.......4

What Is Art?.......................6

Fine Art 8

Part of Culture 10

Art Traditions.................. 12

Sticks and Stones 14

Pottery Art....................... 16

World of Weaving 18

Decorating with Art 20

Notes to Educators 22

Learning More.................23

Glossary and Index 24

Our Global Community

More than 7 billion people live in different countries all around the world. Each country is made up of many **communities**. A community is a group of people who live, work, and play in the same area. You are part of your local community. It includes your home and school. Together, we all belong to one big community—the global community. We all share planet Earth.

tiles, Portugal (page 17)

dreamcatchers, Canada and the United States (page 11)

Different and alike

People in the global community are different in many ways. They are also the same in many ways. Learning about the art that people make around the world helps us see how we are all different and the same in some ways.

In this book, you will learn about art in different places around the world. Many of these places are shown on the map below.

sand paintings, Tibet (page 10)

henna, India (page 13)

basket weaving, Ghana (page 18)

What Is Art?

Art is anything that is made with creativity and skill. Art makes homes and communities more beautiful. It can also make us feel happy, sad, or other ways. There are many kinds of art. This book will show some types of **visual arts** around the world. Visual arts are creations we can look at. They include paintings, drawings, **sculptures**, clothing, and crafts. They do not include dance, music, theater performances, or other types of art.

This ice sculpture in Poland is a type of visual art. We can look at it—until the Sun melts it away!

All kinds of art

People around the world create all kinds of art. Some art has a purpose. Baskets and bowls allow us to hold or carry items. Blankets and clothing cover us and help us stay warm. Other art is made for **decoration**. Decoration is an item put on or around something to make it look nice. We put rugs on our floors. We hang paintings on our walls and fridge doors. It is all beautiful!

Beautiful baskets can be used to carry all kinds of things—even children!

In some places, people decorate their bodies with art. These children in Ethiopia have interesting designs painted on them.

Fine Art

Fine art is art that is created to be beautiful. It doesn't have another use, like clothing or a basket. People around the world have always created fine art. An artist in Italy named Michelangelo made stunning paintings and **statues**. A painter in Mexico named Frida Kahlo created colorful portraits of herself. A French artist named Claude Monet painted lovely pictures of nature. We can see the work of these artists and many others in **museums**.

A museum is a building where special objects, such as art, are kept and shown. These children are visiting a museum in Russia.

Art all around

Not all art is found in museums. Artists build statues in community parks. They make chalk drawings on sidewalks and paint huge murals on buildings. They make mosaics on walls and park benches. Mosaics are pictures made of many small pieces of material, such as stone, tiles, or glass.

Murals are paintings done on walls. This mural is painted on a wall in Scotland.

A tile mosaic brightens up this sign in New York City.

Artists can even carve giant sculptures into the sides of mountains, such as this one on Mount Rushmore, in the United States. It shows four important leaders from that country.

Part of Culture

The art that people make is often part of their **culture**. Culture is a way of life shared by a group of people. It includes their language, food, and **religion**. Many people follow the **Buddhist** religion in an area of Asia called Tibet. Some Buddhists there make colorful sand paintings.

To make sand paintings, artists put colored sand on a design drawn on a table. It can take days to finish.

The artists destroy the art soon after it is done to show their belief that nothing lasts forever.

Catching dreams

Dreamcatchers are part of some **Indigenous** cultures in the United States and Canada. A dreamcatcher is a hoop with strings shaped to look like a spider web. The Ojibwe people began making this type of art long ago. They hung dreamcatchers above their children's beds. An Ojibwe **legend** says that the webs trap bad dreams and keep them away from sleeping children.

dreamcatcher

This Pueblo boy is making a dreamcatcher in New Mexico, United States. The hoop he is holding represents, or stands for, the Sun.

Art Traditions

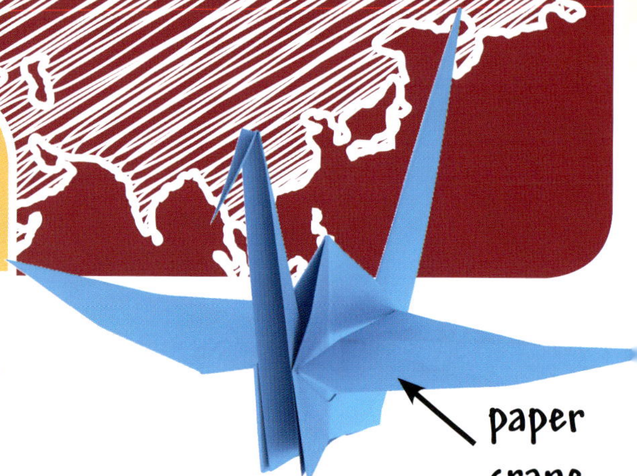

Each culture has its own **traditions**. A tradition is a way of doing things that is passed down from adults to children. People in Japan have been making **origami** sculptures for hundreds of years. Origami is the art of folding paper into shapes. The most common origami shape is of a bird called a crane.

A Japanese legend says that if you fold 1,000 paper cranes, your wish will come true. It is also a tradition to give 1,000 paper cranes as a gift, for good health and luck.

Body art

Some people decorate their bodies as part of their traditions. Most people in India follow the **Hindu** religion. To celebrate weddings, **festivals**, and other special events, women and girls get designs drawn on their hands and feet with a reddish-brown dye called henna.

Many Indigenous peoples in Australia paint their faces and bodies for special events. The colors and designs are traditions passed down from parents. The art represents their tribes, family, and other important things.

Sticks and Stones

People often use the materials found where they live to create art. The Haida, Tsimshian, and other Indigenous peoples who live on the west coast of Canada carve **totem poles** from the tall trees that grow there. Totem poles are sculptures of animals and people. The **Inuit** people who live in Canada's Arctic cannot carve totem poles. Trees do not grow in this frozen part of the world! People there stack rocks to build sculptures.

The sculptures on totem poles show important beliefs, stories, events, and family histories.

This human-shaped Inuit rock sculpture is called an *inuksuk*.

The yarn from alpacas is often used to make **ponchos**, blanket-like coats that have a hole at the top for the wearer's head.

Art supplies

People raise different animals and grow different crops around the world. They can use those **resources** to make art. Some people in Peru raise animals called alpacas. They spin wool from the alpacas to make yarn to create beautiful clothing. People in many countries grow corn to eat. Artists in Slovakia use dry corn husks, or shells, to make dolls.

corn husk doll

Pottery Art

People around the world make **pottery**. Pottery is useful objects, such as bowls and pots, made from **clay**. People form clay into objects with their hands or on a spinning wheel. Then they bake the items so they become hard and sturdy. Some people paint their pottery. Artists in Morocco often make colorful pottery with repeating shapes and designs.

Moroccan pottery

Women in a village in Mali have been making pottery for hundreds of years. They teach their art to their daughters.

The walls of this building in Portugal are covered with beautiful tiles.

Not just pots!

People also use clay to make many other items. Artists in England are known for making fine dishes, vases, dolls, and **figurines**, or small statues. Artists in Portugal are known for making beautiful blue and white tiles. A tile is a thin, flat piece of hard clay. The tiles can be found on walls and floors of homes, churches, and other buildings all around the country!

World of Weaving

People around the world **weave** baskets and other art. Weaving is making an item by crisscrossing strips of material back and forth. Artists often use materials found where they live to create their art. People in villages in northern Ghana make baskets from grass that grows there. People in Thailand use a woody grass called bamboo to weave baskets, hats, rice containers, and other useful items.

Basket weavers in Ghana often dye the grass different colors, then weave it into colorful baskets.

Cloth art

People also weave yarn or threads together to make cloth. They use tools called looms to weave the cloth. The cloth can be used to make rugs, blankets, and other types of art. Weavers in Turkey are known for making beautiful wool carpets. Weavers in China are known for making a fine cloth called silk.

Some artists in China make beautiful designs on the silk.

These Turkish girls and women are practicing the traditional art of carpet weaving.

Decorating with Art

Some types of art are used mainly for decoration. Their purpose is to make spaces look beautiful all year round. Many people use drawings and paintings to decorate their homes. Artists in the Mithila area of India and Nepal are known for their colorful paintings. These drawings used to be painted by women onto the walls and floors of their homes. Today they are also painted on paper and cloth.

Artists dip their fingers, sticks, or brushes into dyes made from plants to create Mithila paintings.

Day of the Dead mask

Holiday art

Some art is made for special holidays that take place in communities each year. Many **Christians** around the world decorate their homes for Christmas. They put up Christmas trees and decorate them with **ornaments** and other art. People in Mexico celebrate the Day of the Dead each fall. Artists make colorful masks, sculptures, and other art to decorate for this fun holiday.

Ornaments are small objects used for decoration. They are a popular type of Christmas art that are often hung on trees.

Notes to Educators

Objective:

This title encourages readers to make global connections by understanding that people around the world express their cultures and traditions by creating art, and that people create art using the materials found in the places where they live.

Main Concepts Include:

- Art is an expression of culture and tradition.
- The methods and materials used, and the purpose for art differs around the world, but people everywhere create art.

Discussion Prompts:

- Revisit the types of art described in this book. Ask readers to identify how different types of art are connected to the environments in which they are made. How do the materials and methods used vary from place to place? How does this compare to art found in their own communities?

Activity Suggestions:

- Invite children to revisit the idea that art is often connected to the cultures and traditions of its artists. Review the examples of cultural or traditional art in this book.
- Ask children to create a piece of visual art that is connected to the culture or traditions of their family or community. Children can decide to create a drawing, a painting, or a statue or sculpture. Provide materials such as paper, paint, colored pencils, clay, small cardboard boxes, craft sticks, tape, glue, pipe cleaners, and other available supplies.
- Guide students by asking them to answer questions such as:
    - How is your piece of art special to you, your family, or your community?
    - Is your piece of art related to any holidays or special events?
    - Did anyone teach you how to create this art? If so, who?
    - Does your art follow any traditions in your family, culture, or community?
- Once completed, invite children to present their art.
- Encourage children to point out how their art connects to their culture or traditions.

Learning More

Books

Abadee, Libby and Armstrong, Cath. *Craft It Up Around the World.* CICO Books, 2013.

Michaels, Alexandra. *The Kids' Multicultural Art Book.* Williamson Books, 2007.

Kuskowski, Alex. *Super Simple Native American Art.* Abdo Publishing Company, 2012.

Websites

http://kids.nationalgeographic.com/explore/wacky-weekend/street-art/#ww-streetart-whale.jpg
This website shows street art from around the world and much more.

www.enchantedlearning.com/crafts/
Learn how to make crafts from Canada, Japan, Mexico, and other countries at this website.

www.enchantedlearning.com/artists/projects.shtml
Visit this website to learn about art and artists from all around the globe.

Glossary

Note: Some **boldfaced** words are defined where they appear in the book.

Buddhist [BOO-diz t] (adjective) To do with Buddhism, a religion based on the teachings of Buddha

Christian [KRIS-chuh n] (noun) A follower of Christianity, a religion based on the teachings of Jesus Christ

clay [kley] (noun) A stiff, sticky type of soil

festival [FES-tuh-vuh l] (noun) An event that is celebrated by a community every year

Hindu [HIN-doo] (adjective) To do with Hinduism, a religion that follows many gods

Indigenous [In-DIJ-en-ous] (adjective) Living naturally in, or native to a place

Inuit [IN-yoo-it] (noun) Indigenous people who live in Northern Canada, Greenland, and the state of Alaska in the United States

legend [LEJ-uh nd] (noun) A story from the past that many people tell and believe but which may not be true

religion [ri-LIJ-uh n] (noun) A set of beliefs and values that people follow and worship

resource [REE-sawrs] Materials, money, or other things that can be used when needed

sculpture [SKUHLP-cher] (noun) An image made of wood, stone, or other solid material

statue [STACH-oo] (noun) A sculpture that shows people or animals the same size or bigger than they are in real life

A noun is a person, place, or thing.
An adjective tells us what something is like.

Index

body painting 7, 13
clay 16-17
decoration 7, 13, 20, 21
global community 4-5
holiday art 21
Indigenous art 11, 12, 14
museum 8-9
origami 12
painting 6-7, 6-8, 10, 13, 16, 20
sculptures 6, 9, 12, 14, 21
tiles 9, 17
weaving 18-19